Get a Clue!

@YOUR LIBRARY

Summer Reading 2007

This book is in honor of

Leila Garcia

for outstanding reading.

Lucy Robbins Welles
LIBRARY

95 Cedar Street, Newington, CT 06111-2645
Voice: 860-665-8700 Children's: 860-665-8720
http://www.newingtonct.gov

WHILE YOU ARE AWAY

By EILEEN SPINELLI

Illustrated by RENÉE GRAEF

HYPERION BOOKS FOR CHILDREN

NEW YORK

Hyperion Books for Children, 114 Fifth Avenue,
New York, New York 10011-5690.
Designed by Christine Kettner
First Edition

1 3 5 7 9 10 8 6 4 2

Reinforced binding
Printed in Singapore
Library of Congress-Cataloging-in-Publication data on file.
ISBN 0-7868-0972-8

Visit www.hyperionchildrensbooks.com

For the children—who wait
—*E.S.*

To Colonel Kevin Benson and all the
servicemen and servicewomen who work with him

A special thank-you to Victoria Benson-Hora
—R.G.

W hile you are on that big ship, Daddy,
far, far away,
I miss you.

I miss going to the farmers' market
on Saturday mornings.
I miss baking brownies,
hunting for salamanders,
collecting river rocks.

While you are on that big ship, Daddy,

far, far away,

I wonder about you.

I wonder: What is my daddy eating for breakfast?

I wonder: Who is bringing chicken soup to my daddy

when he has a cold?

I wonder: Where is my daddy sleeping?

Is he cozy and warm?

While you are on that big ship, Daddy,

far, far away,

I pack things to mail to you:

peanut-butter fudge,

my school picture,

the pot holder I made all by myself.

(Maybe they can use it in the ship's kitchen.)

Dear Dad,
how are
you?

While you are on that big ship, Daddy,
far, far away,
I tell you things.

I pretend the wind can carry my words
clear across the ocean
right to your heart.

I tell you how sometimes I'm scared of the dark.
I tell you how much I love you.
I tell you how much I wish you were here
when you are far, far away.

While you are flying that fast plane, Mommy,

far, far away,

I think about you.

I look up into the big blue sky

and think my happiest thoughts

so you can fly through them as if they are clouds

and smile

and think of me, too.

While you are flying that fast plane, Mommy,
far, far away,

I wrap myself in your old green sweater.

It feels fuzzy and warm.

I play your silver music box

and dance with your pillow.

And when it's bedtime, and the sky is all starry,

I blow kisses to the moon.

Can you catch those kisses, Mommy,

from so far, far away?

While you are flying that fast plane, Mommy,
far, far away,
I dream about you coming home.
In my dream I'm carrying a red balloon
so you can spot me in the crowd.
In my dream you bring me a little bag of presents.
But the very best present of all is you.

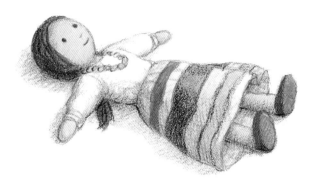

What are you dreaming about, Mommy,
far, far away?

While you are driving that speedy jeep, Papa,

far, far away,

I talk about you.

I bring your photograph to show-and-tell.

I read the letters you send to me. Out loud.

To my pet hamster.

I sing your favorite song to my best friend, Max.

(So what if Max covers his ears!)

While you are driving that speedy jeep, Papa,

far, far away,

I want you to know that

I am taking good care of your garden.

I pull the weeds.

I water the cilantro.

I paint the fence around the roses.

I chase the rabbits. "Shoo!" I say.

"This is my papa's garden!"

While you are driving that speedy jeep, Papa,

far, far away,

I remember what you told me:

Wear your seat belt.

Do your homework.

Give Mama extra hugs.

Don't let the bedbugs bite.

Do you remember what *I* told *you*, Papa?

Keep safe.

Stay well.

Don't get lost driving that speedy jeep,

far, far away.

While you are driving that speedy jeep, Papa,
far, far away,
I wait for the morning Mama will wake me up
and say:
"This is the day!"

The day to turn cartwheels across the living room.
The day to laugh until my tummy aches.
The day to cry a cereal-bowlful of happy tears.
The day to meet you at the station, Papa,
home at last from far, far away.

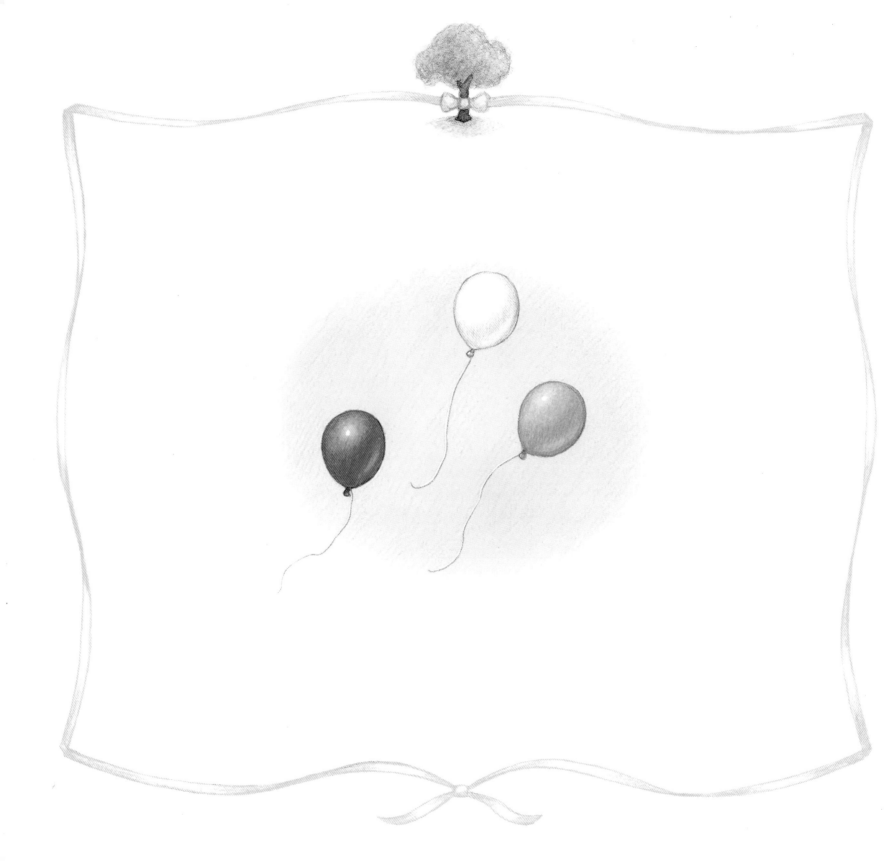